Why The Emu Can't Fly

WRITTEN BY
MAY L. O'BRIEN

ILLUSTRATED BY
SUE WYATT

Sandcastle

FREMANTLE ARTS CENTRE PRESS
CHILDREN'S IMPRINT

Published 1992 by
SANDCASTLE BOOKS
FREMANTLE ARTS CENTRE PRESS
CHILDREN'S IMPRINT
193 South Terrace (PO Box 320), South Fremantle
Western Australia 6162.

First published 1992 Fremantle Arts Centre Press.
Reprinted 1992, 1993

Consultant Editor Alwyn Evans.
Designed by John Douglass.
Production Coordinator Helen Idle.

Typeset in 15/18pt Chelmsford by City Typesetters, West Perth.
Negative preparation by Prepress Services, Perth. Printed on
135gsm Silk Matt and printed by PK Print, Hamilton Hill,
Western Australia.

National Library of Australia Cataloguing-in-publication data

O'Brien, May.
Why the emu can't fly.
ISBN 1 86368 025 X.

[1]. Aborigines, Australian - Legends - Juvenile literature.
[2]. Emus - Folklore - Juvenile literature. I. Title.

398.2245853

This project was assisted by the Aboriginal Arts Committee
of the Australia Council, the Federal Government's
arts funding and advisory body.

Fremantle Arts Centre Press receives financial assistance from
the Western Australian Department for the Arts.

This story, **Why The Emu Can't Fly**, is told in memory of the Wongutha people who lived in the area shown on the map. They helped us to understand that sharing is an important part of community living and that self pride leads to unhappiness.

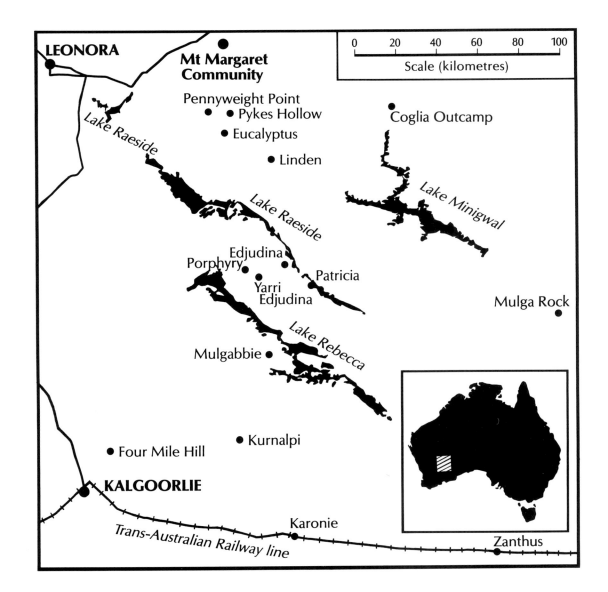

LEONORA

Mt Margaret
Community

Pennyweight Point
Pykes Hollow

Coglia Outcamp

Eucalyptus

Lake Raeside

Linden

Lake Raeside

Lake Minigwal

Edjudina
Porphyry
Patricia

Yarri
Edjudina

Mulga Rock

Lake Rebecca

Mulgabbie

Kurnalpi

Four Mile Hill

KALGOORLIE

Karonie

Trans-Australian Railway line

Zanthus

0   20   40   60   80   100
Scale (kilometres)

INTRODUCTION

These are the stories which were told to children who lived in the area shaded on the map. They are unique to this location. Other groups who lived in different places, have their own language and own stories to tell about how things began. The reason for this, is that the stories came from a time when there was little contact between different groups.

Stories were told so that children would come to understand their land, their people and their beginnings. These stories tell of the animals that shared the land with the people and of how they came into being. Some tell of animals who, through pride, made mistakes and were punished. Others tell of events that help children understand their roles and their responsibilities. The stories had a particular purpose and were important parts of the children's education.

Now, the stories which used to be told can be written, to serve a similar purpose, which is to help today's children understand and appreciate the Aboriginal past as well as the present. *Why The Emu Can't Fly* describes how vanity leads to loss of power and position.

OTHER BOOKS IN THE SERIES

Barn-Barn Barlala, The Bush Trickster tells of children who take no notice of warnings and wander off into the bush. Survival skills learned from their elders help to save them.

How Crows Became Black explains how the crows who were grey, wanted to change colour because no one liked their silver-grey feathers. They felt left out and thought if they were black they would be accepted.

The Kangaroos Who Wanted To Be People tells what happens when walking kangaroos disobey the rules. It helps to explain why some places or areas are out of bounds to children.

At the beginning of time, Wongutha stories tell us that emus could fly. They were the biggest birds in the air and there were many of them. When they flew in their great flocks, they looked like dark clouds moving lazily across the sky.

The emus could see many things happening. They saw the smoke from the people's camp fires as it floated upwards. They watched and laughed as a playful **gubi-gubi** (whirlwind) thrashed through the bush. Twisting and twirling, it gathered up the sticks and leaves in it's path, then tossed them back to the ground.

The emus liked everything they saw and felt pleased with themselves.

Everyone in the bush seemed happy enough. The small birds shared the space in the sky and the animals moved peacefully through the bush.

Because the emus were big and powerful, they felt better than the other birds. Then, things began to change. The emus tossed their heads into the air and became quite snooty. They began to think they were the greatest and fastest birds that ever flew. No one could be better than them, they thought! It wasn't bad to *think* that they were the best, but the emus started to boast about it.

'We can fly higher and faster than anyone else,' they bragged. They looked around to make sure that everyone was looking and listening.

Day after day, week after week and month after month the emus went on with their silly antics. They became even more boastful and the other birds grew tired of them.

The emus became nastier and meaner.

'Let's play a trick on the small birds next time they come flying with us,' they said.

The next morning, the emus were waiting for the other birds. They flew around them, flapping their huge, dusty wings. If that didn't scare the little ones, their next trick did. With wings held high and their heads bent low, their eyes mean and savage, the emus rushed at the small birds. The little birds struggled to stop themselves from crashing into the big, fat emu bullies, who laughed out loud. This bullying went on for a long time, and soon the small birds lost the will to sing. The land became quiet. The people and the animals missed the singing of the birds and wondered why the bush was so silent.

The small birds grew angry with themselves and cried.

'Why do we let the emus do this to us? There must be something we can do to stop them from bullying us.'
They were sad and miserable and they sat in the trees and sulked. The people saw what was happening and they felt sorry for the little birds.

'Garlaya birnigu wiyardu ngurlurri.' (Don't be afraid of the emus.) **'Binangga gulila. Thana yalbrinhba nhurrabanha wandigadigu.'** (Think of some way that you can stop them.)

'We don't know what to do,' replied the birds, 'but one thing is for sure, we've had enough! We're not going to take any more of those stupid tricks from those big fat, bullying birds.'

But, what could small birds do? The emus were too powerful for any little birds.

At last, the birds thought of something that might help them stop the emus bullying. Quickly, they flew off to see the wedge-tailed eagles. The birds found them in a bush clearing, where they were feeding.

'We need your help,' said the small birds nervously. 'We want you to chase the emus out of the sky.' Always ready for a fight, the wedge-tailed eagles agreed to help them.

'We'll ask the hawks to join us,' they said between mouthfuls, while they pulled and tore at their meal.

The eagles and hawks joined forces to try to chase the emus from the sky. However, even this powerful team couldn't defeat the emus. The emus were too big and strong.

When the small birds appeared the next day, the emus mocked and jeered.

'Hah! hah! hah! your measly old plan didn't work, did it? No one can chase *us* out of the sky. Not even the hawks and eagles can do that! We're too smart for them and we're too smart for you!'

In desperation, the unhappy birds turned to the animals for help. The animals sat thinking before they answered.

'We have watched the way the emus behave and we know how well they can fly. We have seen them showing off and we are upset too. But we have to live in the bush with the emus and we don't want to upset them. We're sorry. There's nothing we can do to help you.'

The small birds flew off, angry and upset that the animals had refused to help.

'Our last chance is to ask the pink and grey galahs. They seem to have an answer for everything,' they said to each other. Immediately, they flew off to see them.

The galahs listened to the other birds' story. Then, after a lot of talking amongst themselves, they suggested what they thought was a good idea.

'Really, there's only one thing that you can do,' said the galahs. 'You must wait for the nesting time of the emus. When the eggs have been laid, rush in and crack all of them. Then you won't ever have to worry about the emus again.'

'What a terrible suggestion! We can't do that! We wouldn't like anyone doing that to *our* eggs!' whispered the little birds to each other. 'But, we *are* desperate, and we *must* do something soon. We *will* do as the galahs have suggested.'

The small birds didn't have long to wait for the egg-laying season to begin. When it was time, each of the female emus laid between six and nine big, beautiful, dark green eggs. Then they flew off. It was the male emus' job to sit on the eggs.

'Did you see that? The females have all gone off and left their eggs to the males,' said the surprised little birds.

Every day the small birds sat quietly and patiently in the trees and watched. They were waiting for the emus to take a rest from sitting on the eggs. Finally, the break came. The emus stood up and stretched and moved away.

'Here's our chance,' said the anxious little birds. 'Quickly, get to the eggs and crack them all.' With one swoop, the small birds flew down and stood by the large eggs. The emus saw them and charged back. Terrified, the small birds flew off.

Once again the small birds went to the galahs.

'We tried to do as you said, but we were too afraid of the angry emus,' moaned the little birds.

Feeling ashamed, they turned their heads away and begged, 'Please galahs, do help us again.'

'We've run out of ideas,' replied the galahs in a 'we-can't-be-bothered' tone. 'Go to the older Wongutha men. Those elders will tell you what to do.'

When it was nearly day, the small birds went to the elders.

'Would you please help us get rid of the emus?' asked the small birds. 'They won't share the sky with us anymore.' There was a long pause before the elders answered.

'Garlaya wiyardu mirrindalgu.' (We won't kill the emus.) **'Gugagu guthugu mirrindalgu.'** (We only kill what we need to eat.) **'Bundu yirna yudinthu nhurrabanha wathalgu.'** (But our head man will tell you what to do.) **'Balu ngurra guthubangga nyinarranhi.'** (He is away now.) **'Balu githili gutharrangga ngalalgu.'** (He'll be back in a few months time.) **'Nhurra balugudu wangga.'** (You must talk to him.)

The birds were pleased with the advice that the elders gave and decided to wait in the trees not far away.

A few months later, a messenger came and said that the head man would meet the small birds under the mulga tree. The elder arrived on time. He looked at each one of the little birds. They sensed that he was a very important man and they became quiet.

Speaking in a loud, clear voice, the elder said, **'Ngayulu nhurrabagu balalhgu.'** (I'll help you.) **'Ngayulu garlayagudu durlgu yingagu.'** (I'll sing a special song for the emus.) **'Nhurraba nyina guyula wardangga.'** (You must wait in the trees.) **'Nhurraba balul nyina nhagugu.'** (Then you will see what happens.)

The man looked straight ahead and started to sing in a high-pitched voice. It was an old song from the past, a song handed down by their ancestors to special Wongutha men. The emus heard the singing and flew in from every direction. They gathered around the man and listened.

When the words of the song had faded away, the man turned and disappeared into the bush. For a while the emus just stood there, not knowing what to do or where to turn.

That night, the bush was quiet. Not a sound could be heard. Not even the cicadas or night owls made a noise. While everyone was asleep, something very strange happened to the emus as they ran through the bush in the moonlight. It was very, very strange.

At daybreak, when the emus thought no one was watching, they ran to a clearing in the bush. There, they stretched and flapped their wings to fly away. But nothing happened. Their wings had become stumpy and too small to fly. The emus ran about in panic. They spread their wings and tried to lift off in the breeze. Nothing happened. They tried again and again and again. They stood on a black stump and jumped, thinking that that might help, but still nothing happened. It was useless. The emus were baffled. They questioned each other. Then, they remembered the words of the song, they had heard the day before.

'Garlaya darldu birni, ngayunha gulila.'
(You boastful emus, listen to me.)
'Nhurraba ngula barrbagu, nhurra ngula barrbagu.'
(You won't ever fly again, you won't ever fly again.)
'Ngaba nhurraba dirdu, jinangga barnangga barrabithagu.'
(From now on, you will only walk and run.)

Suddenly, the emus understood the meaning of that special song the important man had sung.

The small birds sitting in the trees had been watching as the emus jumped up and down and flapped about. It was a funny sight. Now, it was the small birds turn to laugh. They laughed so much that they nearly fell off the branches: They began singing and feeling cheerful again.

'Isn't this wonderful? We have the sky to ourselves,' they chirped merrily as they flew up into the open sky. They had room to spread their wings, to swoop, to dive, to glide again. The sky now looked a bigger and brighter place and the air certainly smelt fresh and sweet. The bush was filled with bird songs again, and the birds felt good. It was time for a celebration.

The small birds hurried to thank the Wongutha elders. They told them what had happened. The Wonguthas felt sorry for the emus, but they were pleased that the birds were feeling much happier.

'Garlaya garnbirringu. Thana barrabithanhi ngalibal dawarra.' (One good thing about all of this is that now the emus can wander through the bush with us.) **'Gabi nhanganha burlganha garlayagu, nhurra ngalibagu.'** (This country is big enough for us all.) **'Garlaya birni garnanh-garnanh wiyarringu,'** (The emus have learned not to boast) **'thana yungarra barrabithagu.' (**now they mind their own business.)

PRONUNCIATION GLOSSARY

balu	(ba-lu)	a as in father / u as in put	that person / that one
balugudu	(ba-lu-gu-du)	a as in father / u as in put	to that person
balalgu	(ba-lal-gu)	a as in father / u as in put	do it / make it
balul	(ba-lul)	a as in father / u as in put	in that place / there
balanha	(ba-la-nha)	a as in father / nh dental n	that one
barrbagu	(barr-ba-gu)	a as in father / roll rrs / u as in put	fly
barrabithagu	(barr-a-bith-a-gu)	a as in father / roll rrs i as in it / u as in put	walk around roam around
barrabithanhi	(ba-rra-bith-anh-i)	a as in father / roll rrs nh dental n / i as in it	walking around roaming around
barnangga	(barn-ang-ga)	a as in father / rn retroflex n ng as in sing	on / in the ground
binangga	(bin-ang-ga)	i as in it / a as in father ng as in sing	listen with your ears
birni	(birn-i)	i as in it / retroflex rn	those / many
birnigu	(birn-i-gu)	i as in it / rn retroflex rn	for them
bundu	(bun-du)	u as in put	man
burlganha	(burl-ga-nha)	u as in put / rl retroflex l a as in father / nh dental n	important one boss person / big boss
dawarra	(da-warr-a)	a as in father / roll rrs	with us / as well
darldu	(darl-du)	a as in father / rl retroflex l / u as in put	proud / snooty / haughty
dirdu	(dird-u)	i as in it / rd retroflex d u as in put	continue / forever
durlgu	(durl-gu)	u as in put / retroflex rl	sing / song
gabi	(ga-bi)	a as in father / i as in it	water / country
garlaya	(garl-a-ya)	a as in father / retroflex rl u as in put	emu
garlayagu	(garl-a-ya-gu)	a as in father / retroflex rl	for the emus
garlayagudu	(garl-a-ya-gu-du)	a as in father / u as in put / retroflex rl	to the emus
garnanh-garnanh	(garn-anh-garn-anh)	a as in father / retroflex rn nh dental n	snooty / boastful haughty / arrogant

garnbirringu	(garn-birr-ing-u)	a as in father / retroflex rn roll rrs / ng as in sing / u as in put	got better / became better / improved
githili	(gi-thi-li)	i as in it	moon
gubi-gubi	(gu-bi-gu-bi)	u as in put / i as in it	whirlwind / small spiralling upward wind, also called a willy-willy.
gugagu	(gu-ga-gu)	u as in put / a as in father	meat
gulila	(gu-li-la)	u as in put / i as in it / a as in father	listen
guthugu	(gu-thu-gu)	u as in put	one / one and only
gutharrungga	(gu-tharr-ung-ga)	u as in put / a as in father roll rrs / ng as in sing	two
guthubangga	(gu-thu-bang-ga)	u as in put / a as in father ng as in sing	another place the other way
guyula	(gu-yu-la)	u as in put / a as in father	wait
jinangga	(ji-nang-ga)	i as in it / a as in father ng as in sing	on one's feet with one's feet
ngaba	(nga-ba)	ng as in sing / a as in father	therefore / instead
nhagugu	(nha-gu-gu)	nh dental n / a as in father u as in put	see
ngalalgu	(nga-lal-gu)	ng as in sing / a as in father u as in put	will come
nhananha	(nha-na-nha)	nh dental n / a as in father ng as in sing	this one
ngayunha	(nga-yu-nha)	ng as in sing / a as in father u as in put	me
ngalibal	(nga-li-bal)	a as in father / ng as in sing i as in it	with all of us with us
ngalibagu	(nga-li-ba-gu)	ng as in sing / a as in father i as in it / u as in up	ours
ngayulu	(nga-yu-lu)	ng as in sing / a as in father u as in put	I did / I will
ngula	(ngu-la)	ng as in sing / u as in put a as in father	will not / won't
nyina	(nyi-na)	ny dental n / i as in it / a as in father	sit / stay
nyinarranhi	(nyi-narr-a-nhi)	ny dental y / i as in it a as in father / roll rrs	sitting staying

ngulurri	(ngu-lurr-i)	ng as in sing / u as in put roll rrs / i as in it	afraid of becoming afraid
ngurra	(ngu-rra)	ng as in sing / u as in put roll rrs / a as in father	home / place
nhurra	(nhu-rra)	nh dental n / u as in put roll rrs / a as in father	you
nhurraba	(nhu-rra-ba)	nh dental n / u as in put roll rrs / a as in father	you lot all of you
nhurrabagu	(nhu-rra-ba-gu)	nh dental n / u as in put roll rrs / a as in father	for all of
nhurrabanha	(nhu-rra-ba-nha)	nh dental n / u as in put roll rrs / a as in father	you lot all of you
mirrindalgu	(mi-rrin-dal-gu)	i as in it / roll rrs a as in father / u as in put	kill
thana	(tha-na)	a as in father	them / they
wandigadigu	(wan-di-ga-di-gu)	a as in father / i as in it / u as in put	will leave alone
wangga	(wang-ga)	ng as in sing / a as in father	talk to / speak to
wardangga	(ward-ang-ga)	retroflex rd / a as in father	by the tree
wathalgu	(wa-thal-gu)	a as in father / u as in put	tell
wiyardu	(wi-yard-u)	i as in it / a as in father retroflex rd / u as in put	won't
wiyarringu	(wi-yarr-ing-u)	i as in it / a as in father / roll rrs ng as in sing / u as in put	gone
Wongutha	(Wong-u-tha)	short vowel sound o / ng as in sing u as in up / a as in father	name of the Aboriginal people from the Eastern Goldfields of WA
yarlbrinhba	(yarl-brinh-ba)	a as in father / rl retroflex l i as in it / nh dental n	how think of some way?
yirna	(yirn-a)	i as in it / rn retroflex n a as in father	head person / boss
yingagu	(yin-ga-gu)	i as in it / a as in father u as in put	sing
yudinthu	(yu-din-thu)	u as in put / i as in it	he will tell you straight
yungarra	(yung-arr-a)	u as in put / ng as in sing a as in father / roll rrs	alone by themselves